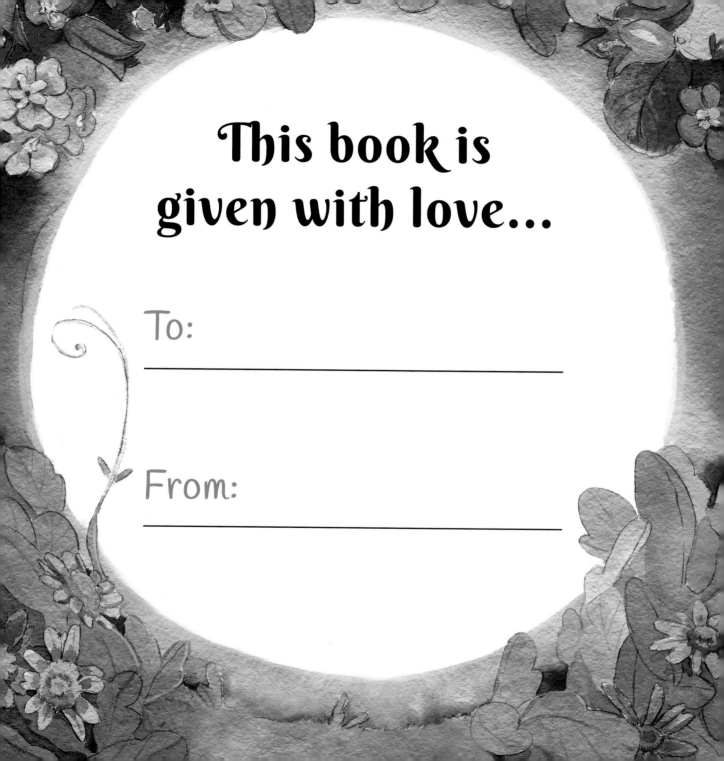

This book is given with love...

To:

_____

From:

_____

This story is for my parents.
Your love has always been
the greatest gift.

– Meryl Davis

Written by
Meryl Davis

Illustrated by
Evgeniya Kozhevnikova

Moon Walk
Forever By Your Side

Tonight let's walk,
Together through the stars...

A "Moon Walk" we call it,
This special time of ours.

Your sweet little hand,
Wrapped so tightly in mine...

I woke you from slumber,
To see what we could find.

The crescent moon above,
The stars shining bright...

Darling, don't forget:

This magic, this moment,
This memory... just right!

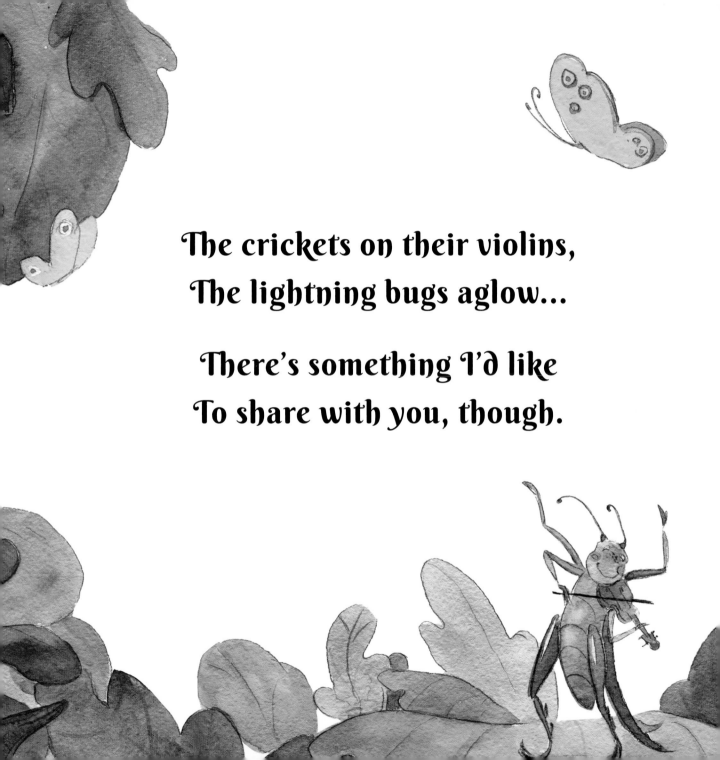

The crickets on their violins,
The lightning bugs aglow...

There's something I'd like
To share with you, though.

For you, I dream of kindness,
Of beauty, and of peace...

But life can surprise us,
To say the very least.

So let's keep walking,
I'll listen as we go...

Share your heart with me,
Let your feelings show.

There will be times of celebration,
Of dancing, and of joy...

But some challenges, too,
For every girl and boy.

You can tell me anything,
I am on your team...

No matter how confusing,
Or difficult it may seem.

You are never alone,
I'm forever by your side...

To cherish your laugh,
Or hold you as you cry.

If you're facing an issue,
Or life's been unfair...

Let the stars remind you,
Just how much I care.

I'll be here for you,
I hope you know...

Ready to listen
As you learn, change, and grow.

Nothing can stop that,
You're stuck with me, kid...

No matter what you say,
Think, feel, or did.

So, let's keep chatting,
As we walk through the stars...

The sky is the limit,
And this time is ours.

I'll always love you,
And will hold you tight...

And forever treasure,
Each magical "Moon Walk" night.

The End

About the Author

Meryl Davis grew up in the suburbs of Detroit, Michigan with her loving parents, Cheryl and Paul Davis, and younger brother, Clayton. Indeed, "Moon Walks" were a magical part of Meryl's childhood and are still a cherished family tradition. After standing atop the Olympic podium in 2014 with her longtime partner, Charlie White, Meryl traveled the world with several international figure skating tours as she completed her undergraduate degree in anthropology at the University of Michigan; all while dreaming of her next adventure. Meryl currently resides in Los Angeles, California with her husband, Fedor, and their miniature sheepadoodle, Bilbo, who loves cuddles and playing fetch on the beach more than just about anything.

Claim your FREE Gift!
PDICBooks.com/Gift

Thank you for purchasing a copy of Moon Walk
and welcome to the Puppy Dogs & Ice Cream family.
We're certain you're going to love the little gift
we've prepared for you at the website above.